Samuel French Acting Edition

I0591829

Advice From a Caterpillar

A Comedy in Two Acts

by Douglas Carter Beane

SAMUELFRENCH.COM   SAMUELFRENCH.CO.UK

Copyright © 1991 by Douglas Carter Beane
All Rights Reserved

ADVICE FROM A CATERPILLAR is fully protected under the copyright laws of the United States of America, the British Commonwealth, including Canada, and all other countries of the Copyright Union. All rights, including professional and amateur stage productions, recitation, lecturing, public reading, motion picture, radio broadcasting, television and the rights of translation into foreign languages are strictly reserved.

ISBN 978-0-573-69294-9

www.SamuelFrench.com
www.SamuelFrench.co.uk

FOR PRODUCTION ENQUIRIES

UNITED STATES AND CANADA
Info@SamuelFrench.com
1-866-598-8449

UNITED KINGDOM AND EUROPE
Plays@SamuelFrench.co.uk
020-7255-4302

Each title is subject to availability from Samuel French, depending upon country of performance. Please be aware that *ADVICE FROM A CATERPILLAR* may not be licensed by Samuel French in your territory. Professional and amateur producers should contact the nearest Samuel French office or licensing partner to verify availability.

CAUTION: Professional and amateur producers are hereby warned that *ADVICE FROM A CATERPILLAR* is subject to a licensing fee. Publication of this play(s) does not imply availability for performance. Both amateurs and professionals considering a production are strongly advised to apply to Samuel French before starting rehearsals, advertising, or booking a theatre. A licensing fee must be paid whether the title(s) is presented for charity or gain and whether or not admission is charged. Professional/ Stock licensing fees are quoted upon application to Samuel French.

No one shall make any changes in this title(s) for the purpose of production. No part of this book may be reproduced, stored in a retrieval system, or transmitted in any form, by any means, now known or yet to be invented, including mechanical, electronic, photocopying, recording, videotaping, or otherwise, without the prior written permission of the publisher. No one shall upload this title(s), or part of this title(s), to any social media websites.

For all enquiries regarding motion picture, television, and other media rights, please contact Samuel French.

MUSIC USE NOTE

Licensees are solely responsible for obtaining formal written permission from copyright owners to use copyrighted music in the performance of this play and are strongly cautioned to do so. If no such permission is obtained by the licensee, then the licensee must use only original music that the licensee owns and controls. Licensees are solely responsible and liable for all music clearances and shall indemnify the copyright owners of the play(s) and their licensing agent, Samuel French, against any costs, expenses, losses and liabilities arising from the use of music by licensees. Please contact the appropriate music licensing authority in your territory for the rights to any incidental music.

IMPORTANT BILLING AND CREDIT REQUIREMENTS

If you have obtained performance rights to this title, please refer to your licensing agreement for important billing and credit requirements.

This play is dedicated to Mike Rosenberg, for giving me the freedom to write it. And Ed Lansbury, for giving me the courage to rewrite it.

The first draft of *Caterpillar* was written in two weeks on a dare by Mike Rosenburg to fill the fall slot of his college's "experimental theatre." In October '89, at James Madison University under the direction of Michael Rosenburg and stage management of Megan Dolan the play was performed with Paul Lord, Christian Holloway, Patrick McClellend and the magnificent Janice O'Rourke.

I did some rewrites. It was then optioned for production by Edgar Lansbury. I did some rewrites. A reading was done in New York in April '90 with Billy DeAquitis, Tony Cummings, Michael Ornstein and Jessica Tuck. I did some rewrites.

In August '90, *Caterpillar* made its professional debut when American Theatre Works (Jill Charles, artistic director, John Nassivera, producing director) presented the Dorset Theatre Festival production. Sets by Wm. John Aupperlee, costumes by Eric Hansen, lighting and sound by Jeffrey Bernstein, stage management by Carol Dawes, direction by Edgar Lansbury, with the following cast:

Missy	Jennie Moreau
Suit	Harley Venton
Spaz	Eric Swanson
Brat	Michael Ornstein
Voice of Linda Lee	Monica Tecca

Yeah. I did some rewrites. And with each of these rewrites many have helped me. In addition to everyone mentioned above, I give my gratitude to: Jonathan Bixby, Peter Buck, Carol Channing, John and Karen Clift, Steve Flaherty, Greg Gale, Frank Gallagher, Earl Graham, Ching Gonzales, Deb Hall, Martin Hynes, Don, Diane and C.J. Kendall, Gretchen Krich, Rose Lansbury, John Edward McGrath, Randolph Miles, David Robbins, David Semonin, Charlotte Sheedy, Keith Sherman, Bob White.

v

With the New York production, I did more rewrites with the help of everyone in that cast and crew (from the brilliant leading lady on down). After the New York production, I stopped. It's just time to write another play.

Advice From a Caterpillar was presented on April 4th, 1991 at the Lucille Lortel Theatre, New York City, by John Nassivera and Don Schneider by special arrangement with Lucille Lortel. The play was directed by Edgar Lansbury, scenery by Rick Dennis, costumes by Jonathan Bixby, lighting by Brian Nason, original music by David Abir, stage management by Robert Bennett. The cast was as follows :

Missy...Ally Sheedy
Suit...Harley Venton
Spaz..Dennis Christopher
Brat...David Lansbury
Voice of Linda Lee...................................Gretchen Krich

CHARACTERS

Missy   She, like the others in the cast, is in her late twenties. An East Village artist, currently working in video. Attractive, with an exciting and exotic style of dress, her sarcastic sense of humor is undercut by her charm and good spirits.

Spaz   An East Village performance artist. Gay. Handsome, intelligent and trendily stylish. Despite an almost surreal sense of humor, he is very "down to earth."

Suit   An investment banker. A W.A.S.P. of the "old boy" network. His conservative speech and clothing is a contrast to the downtowners. Handsome.

Brat   An East Village actor, specializing in Brecht and German Expressionists. An Italian-American "Jersey boy," well-built and good looking, his style is more "cool" than Spaz's "dandy."

TIME

The present

PLACE

Act I — Various locations, New York City's East Village
Act II — A country house, Old Chatham, New York

MUSIC

During the twelve scene changes of the first act, hip-hop music should blare and the actors should casually dance into place

AUTHOR'S NOTE

The first act set changes in the New York production were filled with music and movement. In no way feel obliged to recreate moving platforms. A unit set can be used with visible stage hands carrying on minimalist bits of furniture. Projections can flash on names of locations. Just keep the movement, the dancing and the music. It emphasizes the last moment of each scene—important in building the events that change Missy's life. The score by David Abir is wonderful and can be obtained from Priceless Recordings (212) 254-5201. If not, a collection of hip-hop or house may be used. Dee-Lite's *World Clique* has the right feel.

Please note:

Mention is made of songs which are *not* in the public domain. Producers of this play are hereby CAUTIONED that permission to produce this play does not include rights to use these songs in production. Producers should contact the copyright owners directly for rights.

ACT I

Scene 1

Missy's bedroom.

MISSY. Have you ever been in love?

SUIT. (*Pause.*) Oh Jesus.

MISSY. What?

SUIT. That question.

MISSY. What "that question"?

SUIT. That is quite the obvious post-coital question.

MISSY. Am I being cliché? I hate it when I'm cliché.

SUIT. Why do you ask?

MISSY. If I'm being cliché?

SUIT. No, if I've been in love.

MISSY. Curious.

SUIT. Are you falling in love with me?

MISSY. Please. (*Pause.*) Oh please.

SUIT. I don't know. Love? Maybe when I was in college once.

MISSY. You love your daughter?

SUIT. Lizbeth? Of course. But that's not in love.

MISSY. Right. Your wife?

SUIT. (*Thinks about it.*) God. Yes. Of course. At times.

MISSY. Me?

SUIT. Do you want me to be?

MISSY. Get a clue.

SUIT. Are you feeling guilt about us?
MISSY. Guilt. Dear. That's real—
SUIT. What?
MISSY. Quaint.
SUIT. Guilt is quaint, isn't it?

(THEY kiss.)

SUIT. I had fun.
MISSY. Likewise, I'm sure.
SUIT. I have to get dressed. The conference I bagged will be over in half an hour. They'll be expecting me.
MISSY. Shame. I like being naked with you. It's the only time we have things in common. Dressed, we do not look good together.
SUIT. Why not?
MISSY. I don't know. You're such the suit. I'm such the not. Sex is like what we have in common.
SUIT. *(Getting dressed.)* You mean our ... "affair."
MISSY. *(Laughing.)* The word.
SUIT. I know.
MISSY. Can you even?
SUIT. Our "affair." And I'm a ... "cheat." And you're my "mistress."
MISSY. Am not.
SUIT. Are too.
MISSY Am not. If I was your "mistress," I would be kept. You don't keep me. I keep myself. At best I'm the "other woman."
SUIT. You know what you are Missy?
MISSY. What?
SUIT. You're "modern."

MISSY. Fuck you.

SUIT. You're a "modern gal."

MISSY. Right. I'm Ann Romano.

SUIT. Who?

MISSY "One Day at a Time."

SUIT. Sitcom?

MISSY. Right.

SUIT. Rich white guy adopts poor black kids?

MISSY. No. God. Suit, have you ever like not read a book? "One Day at a Time." Bonnie Franklin as Ann Romano. Divorced woman raising two daughters in a seventies sitcom. And they have a kooky super. And she's a modern gal.

SUIT. Right right.

MISSY. They show the reruns weekdays at four on eleven.

SUIT. Great.

MISSY. Patronizing. Anyway, I watched it last Thursday. Ann went away for the weekend with a married man.

SUIT. Oooh.

MISSY. She couldn't put out.

SUIT. Aaaaah.

MISSY. She saw the photos of the wife and kiddies and got but wigged. Ann is a modern gal but she has an inner sense of morality.

SUIT. And what did you think of Ann's inner sense of morality?

MISSY. It went very well with her cowl neck and gauchos.

SUIT. You're a serious madwoman.

(THEY kiss.)

    MISSY. Do you love me?
    SUIT. No.
    MISSY. Good.
    SUIT. See you Tuesday.

Scene 2

SPAZ's kitchen.

    SPAZ. That video of yours is the highlight of the show. Next to the animated film of the Betty Ford story. The one told entirely with G.I. Joes.
    MISSY. Thanks. I should take it in.
    SPAZ. It's only the Whitney. You're only in it. Gee, you think?
    MISSY. Whitney branch.
    SPAZ. You're in it, you should see it. The entrance is to seriously die. You walk in, big sign, "Suburbia in Art." And on the first big wall. Huge oversized photos of Levittown. We all just stood there speechless, transfixed. We refugees of America's suburbs living in the like bowels of New York now. There must have been like twenty different styles of tract house on the wall.
    MISSY. Wow.
    SPAZ. Now I know how Jews feel looking at Chagall. You should go. Just for the aesthetics.
    MISSY. Please.
    SPAZ. The networking, then.

MISSY. I've got a new system. Anti-networking. I don't go places where my work is. It implies I'm too big for the show altogether.

SPAZ. This is why your career is soaring and I'm in the proverbial nowheresville.

MISSY. You're not in nowheresville. You're a performance artist. Of like note.

SPAZ. No, Missy, I'm worse than that. I'm an old performance artist. Who does other people's pieces. And I've been around so long that now the pressure could not be on me more. To create my own pieces. Or cater.

MISSY. Spaz. I'm going to smack you.

SPAZ. I am old, Father William.

MISSY. You are like late twenties.

SPAZ. For a career person and not a success, that is old.

MISSY. Stop.

SPAZ. I mean what should be like giving my life purpose? Love? I think not.

MISSY. So create a performance piece.

SPAZ. It's not in me.

MISSY. It's in you.

SPAZ. Missy, don't get queen of whatever with me, I'm like quite sure you're going to understand my dilemma. You who just but has it all. Career on the rise and boyfriend.

MISSY. I do not have a boyfriend.

SPAZ. What about the Suit?

MISSY. The Suit is a married man I have the sex with.

SPAZ. Is the sex good?

MISSY Forget it.

SPAZ. I resent you.

MISSY. I mean like, excuse me, but did I just scream the wallpaper off the wall in ecstasy there or what?

SPAZ. I want your life. A career and an uncomplicated relationship.

MISSY. It's not—there are threats of complications all the time. Like I honestly worry that my married man will turn out to be the Big "L."

SPAZ. The big "L"?

MISSY The big "L."

SPAZ. Wait a minute, I'm confused. You're worried because you think your married man might turn out to be Elvis?

MISSY. No.

SPAZ. Elvis is dead, Missy.

MISSY. Spaz.

SPAZ. I know, I know, you mean love.

MISSY. It's a legitimate fear.

SPAZ. Our work is supposed to be influenced by suburbia, not our lives. I mean, like love? I'm so sure.

MISSY. Thank you.

SPAZ. I mean like skipping in woods and singing Partridge Family songs? And then one day getting unrequited and suffering? I'm not.

MISSY. Excuse me. Thank you.

SPAZ. And making a big, beautiful fool of yourself.

MISSY. Now you're being like overly dramatic.

SPAZ. Excuse me? Wait. (*Exits, returns with a pottery vase.*) A big, beautiful fool.

MISSY. What is that?

SPAZ. What does it look like?

MISSY. Something from the lesbian pinchware collective?

SPAZ. No, Missy, this is like exhibit A in love makes a big, beautiful fool of you. This, dare I call it, "piece" is not a vase. Oh no, it is an actual signed piece of art. Created for me by some boy that I actually made the incredible fool mistake of loving. I ... inspired this piece.

MISSY. No.

SPAZ. It was the seventies, be kind.

MISSY. Sorry.

SPAZ. It's embarrassing. But what's even more embarrassing, I can't throw the butt-ugly thing out. It like makes its way to the trash can any number of times and I just remember like George the silly seventies pottery guy who made it and how we would be like seventeen like get naked and smoke pot and listen to Joni Mitchell and have wallpaper-tearing sex and ... whatever. So I have to keep it. Not out. It's hidden in a cabinet. But I keep it.

MISSY. Would you want to love again?

SPAZ. Excuse me, no.

MISSY. I mean, I wouldn't ... want to be in love.

SPAZ. I mean I'd like to have a boyfriend. Someone cute to go places with and who would help me with crosswords, but like—

MISSY. Love?

SPAZ. Love? I'm so not.

MISSY. Oh, Spaz. Are we cynical?

SPAZ. Are you kidding? I consider that my best trait.

Scene 3

A radio station.

MISSY. (*Wearing earphones, SHE tentatively speaks into the microphone.*) Uhm ... hello?

VOICE OF LINDA. (*Heard but not seen.*) Have you ever been on radio before?

MISSY. Uh ... no.

V.O.L. (VOICE OF LINDA.) No problem. Just talk amiably into your microphone and pretend we're old friends.

MISSY. Where are you?

V.O.L. Washington, D.C.

MISSY. Could we do this possibly in the same state?

V.O.L. We need a sound check. Just say two words into your microphone. Any two words.

MISSY. (*After some consideration.*) Farrah Fawcett-Majors.

V.O.L. That's three words.

MISSY. The last two are hyphenated.

V.O.L. (*Dripping with sarcasm.*) Great. We're going to have fun. I just love talking to artists.

MISSY. Could we do this interview looking at each —

(Too late. The intro has started. Bach and a VOICE OVER.)

VOICE OVER. And now National Public Radio presents "artspeak." And here's your host for "artspeak," Linda Lee.

(MISSY mouths the name "Linda Lee" incredulously.)

VOICE OVER. Linda?

V.O.L. Hi! I'm chatting this afternoon with hip downtown artist Missy. Missy?

MISSY. Here.

V. O.L. Please explain your work to our home listeners.

MISSY. Well ... uhm ... Linda Lee ... Uh, like there is nothing a creative person loves more than like explaining his or her self-explanatory work. The piece that's currently at the Whitney branch is entitled, "Birthdays—Birth to Present." It is a video of mine. It is a chronological study of my birthdays taken from home movies that were taken by my father. So I got the idea of showing my parties back to back in order and then filming my latest birthday. I transferred the film to video. And there was no sound, so I narrated it and uh, so, that was that piece.

V.O.L. Sounds hip. What does your mother think of your work?

MISSY. Subtle sexism there, Linda Lee. Don't think you'd dream of asking Julian Schnabel what his dad thought of his work. To answer the question—She likes it. Well, I mean, she lives in suburban Pennsylvania, so much is lost on her, but she like comes to my openings with Dad and has a good time. And she's supportive and like insightful. In the piece I just mentioned, "Birthdays," for example, she was actually the first person to notice the similarities between my Aunt Theresa at my second party and the drag queen at my latest party.

V.O.L. Sounds hip. Tell me, do you believe the hype?

MISSY. Constantly.

V. O. L. What other works do you have in the home movies series?

MISSY. Uh, in the the home movies series, there's "Wildwood '63 to '72," which is a look at my family's vacations in Wildwood, New Jersey. "Dates," which is the compilation of footage my dad had made of me leaving before each of my dates up to and including the Prom. Dad filmed everything. And then the latest in the series, "Christmas Trees—Aluminum to pine." Which is self-explanatory ... not that that means anything this afternoon.

V.O.L. I saw "Dates" on P.B.S. "Alive From Off Center." You say such mean things in your commentary in that film.

MISSY. Well ... mean? I don't know, how about ironic? Isn't everybody ironic anymore? I mean, can anyone still introduce their boyfriend as their boyfriend without putting quotes and an aware sneer around it? Aren't our favorite jokes the cruel ones? Aren't the rude talk show hosts the ones we think are funny?

V.O.L. Insightful. And hip. How do you like being labeled "Post-Modern"?

MISSY. I like it. I like it just fine. These questions are great. I can only imagine what you look like.

V.O.L. On a personal note, whatever happened to the boy from "Dates"? The prom date?

MISSY. God. Right. Mickey today is, as far as I know, married and living in Pennsylvania. I think he's a lawyer, I don't keep in touch. It's not like I—he wasn't a love or anything. I've been very lucky. (*A pause. SHE thinks about what she's just said.*)

Scene 4

Spaz's kitchen.

MISSY. Is that the last of the capons please say yes?

SPAZ. Maybe we should take a break.

MISSY. Maybe you shouldn't take catering jobs before you're ready and call best friends in tears and make them drop everything and come over and help you.

SPAZ. Please. Tear my head off, will you? But first let's have a coffee break. Wash your hands.

MISSY. I'm complaining to the shop steward. You're running a pesto scented sweat shop.

(SHE exits, HE gets out the coffee, SHE returns.)

SPAZ. Coffee's on the table.

MISSY. Before I take so much as a sip, please tell me, who is the nude boy in your bedroom?

SPAZ. God. Completely forgot. Potential new boyfriend. Cream and sugar are here.

MISSY. First time?

SPAZ. The only first time. Adam and Eve did not have this first a time. I have Sweet and Low.

MISSY. Great. Did you play safe?

SPAZ. Very.

MISSY. How safe?

SPAZ. Any safer and we wouldn't have been in the same room.

MISSY. Not prying, just concerned. Good coffee.

SPAZ. Thanks for the concern, thanks for the compliment. Croissant?

MISSY. Please. What's his name?

SPAZ. Tony.

MISSY. Tony. Let me guess. Italian?

SPAZ. Very Italian.

MISSY. My, my. Italian this time. You really are working your way through the United Colors of Benetton.

SPAZ. Bitch. Jelly? So what did you think of him?

MISSY. Spaz. I saw him nude asleep on a comforter.

SPAZ. What did you think?

MISSY. The only thing I could judge him on is physical appearance.

SPAZ. That's O.K. What's the first thing that popped into your head?

MISSY. The first thing was "Girl, get a look at that institution over there."

SPAZ. An institution?

MISSY. A major institution.

SPAZ. How major the institution?

MISSY. Sears will paint him.

SPAZ. But it's more than a physical thing.

MISSY. Who cares?

SPAZ. He's a nice guy.

MISSY. Is it love? (*Indicating croissant.*) Did you make these?

SPAZ. "Yes" to croissant, "no" to love. Not even a threat of it. Turns out he's ... Bi.

MISSY. A bisexual. God, how seventies.

SPAZ. I know.

MISSY. I didn't know they still made those.

SPAZ. I'm loaning my new boyfriend and my vase to the Smithsonian for their display on the Carter Administration.

MISSY. Lucky you. New career and loveless boyfriend. Lucky lucky you.

SPAZ. I tell you, the second my bi guy starts getting mushy, I'll just say, "wouldn't you rather be with a woman?" Do we know our safety nets? You with married man, me with bisexual. I have marmalade if you'd rather.

MISSY. I'm fine. Quick question.

SPAZ. Yeah?

MISSY. Why is not new boyfriend out here helping with catering deadline?

SPAZ. It's a new relationship, I don't want to put demands on him right away.

MISSY. What? And you can drag my ass over here to do it? Fuck you; no really. Bring him out here. Right now.

SPAZ. He's sleepi—

MISSY. Hey, Tony!!!

SPAZ. His nickname is Brat.

MISSY. Hey, Bra—Brat???

SPAZ. I know. Flawless.

MISSY. Hey, Brat!

SPAZ. Missy, you are dee-ranged.

MISSY. Spaz, you are dee-mented.

SPAZ. I thought I was Dee-gorgeous!

BRAT. (*Enters wearing a comforter.*) Hi. Coffee?

SPAZ. Brat, this is Missy. Missy, this is Brat.

BRAT. Hi.

MISSY. Hi.

(*THEY shake hands.*)

Scene 5

Missy's Bedroom.

MISSY. And he seems nice.

SUIT. Good for Spaz. What's his name?

MISSY. Brat.

SUIT. What's that about?

MISSY. Don't know. Couldn't be nicer. Maybe just that he's cute and knows it.

SUIT. Conceited?

MISSY. No, he knows he's cute like he doesn't worry about it, not like he knows he's cute and relishes it.

SUIT. What does he do?

MISSY. Sexually? I've no idea.

SUIT. No, I mean do. A career. Everyone has a career.

MISSY. He's an actor-type.

SUIT. An actor who isn't conceited?

MISSY. It happens. He's real—what's important is that I think he's real good for Spaz.

SUIT. What kind of an actor?

MISSY. Eccentric taste.

SUIT. How eccentric?

MISSY. He likes Brecht.

SUIT. What's Brecht?

MISSY. It would only upset you.

SUIT. So are he and Spaz "in love"?

MISSY. Nah. I mean, a struggling actor and a performance artist turning caterer? They're so busy. Who's going to have time for love?

SUIT. Right.

MISSY. They've got so much —

SUIT. Exactly.

MISSY. To concentrate on.

SUIT. Right. I think I have to orchestrate a departure right now.

MISSY. Oh.

SUIT. It's getting late.

MISSY. Stay a little bit—uhm—never mind. Right. It is late.

SUIT. I can stay longer.

MISSY. I mean if that's what you want.

SUIT. How's work?

MISSY. Tough ... satisfying ... whatever. Big, beautiful whatever.

SUIT. What are you working on?

MISSY. Another video. Sifting through home movies for shots of appliances. How do you feel about appliances?

SUIT. Good. I feel good about appliances.

MISSY. How long you going to be away?

SUIT. That again?

MISSY. Again? This is the first time I brought it up.

SUIT. Three weeks. It's an emergency.

MISSY. An emergency that requires a banker? Someone need singles?

SUIT. You're unhappy.

MISSY. Maybe. I'm ... not happy, Suit.

SUIT. There's not much I can do about that. I could divorce Jan and run off with you. But that's very drastic.

MISSY. God, you bring that up. All the time. Please. For me. As a favor. Do not even consider that.

SUIT. Stranger things have happened.

MISSY. Aren't you happy as things are?

SUIT. Happy? What are—(*A moment.*) Who am I to complain? People have got it much worse than me.

MISSY. Do you ever worry about the big stuff?

SUIT. What, the G.N.P.?

MISSY. No, like feelings of emptiness?

SUIT. I try not to think about shit like that.

MISSY. Shit like that has been filling me with despair lately. I hate myself, I think.

SUIT. Why do you hate yourself? *The Times* loves your work.

MISSY. Suit, you are classic.

SUIT. I have to go. Is there anything I can do to make you happy?

MISSY. No.

SUIT. Sure you're not mad at me?

MISSY. Why?

SUIT. Because I'm going away for two weeks.

MISSY. Three. No.

SUIT. Good. I have to go.

MISSY. Bye.

SUIT. Bye.

MISSY. Suit?

SUIT. Yes?

MISSY. Do I give you happiness?

SUIT. No. But you do distract me from unhappiness.

Scene 6

A Soho gallery.

BRAT. (*Spotting MISSY, who is staring with disbelief at a huge photograph of her face emblazoned with the words "Missy: a retrospective."*) Missy! You're a hit.

MISSY. Hey, Brat.

BRAT. Your work is, Oh God, It is like—BLAM!

MISSY. Oh yeah?

BRAT. No really. I am just frothing here. It is SO amazing. I mean, I don't mean to be gushing all over you but—

MISSY. No, please gush.

BRAT. It's so powerful and meaningful and it says so much and—Now I don't know anything about art. Please. If I knew any less about art, I'd be a congressman, right?

MISSY. (*Charmed.*) Right.

BRAT. But, this stuff is so intense. I don't know why everybody is so glum and talking about dinner and stuff. I mean this is—I haven't felt this worked about stuff in a gallery since—I don't mean to compare you to another artist —

MISSY. Go ahead.

BRAT. But I haven't felt this excited since ... Well, I would put your work in the same league as ... The Helga paintings.

MISSY. (*A moment. WE see that this is an unintended slap in the face.*) Oh really. The Hel—all of them?

BRAT. Oh yeah.

MISSY. Thanks. Uhm—Where's Spaz?

BRAT. He's over by the white wine and cheese being bitter. He hates his life tonight. I mean it, Missy. The Helga paintings.

MISSY. I may cry.

BRAT. So What are you going to do next?

MISSY. I'm interested in maintaining my pursuit of an ironic view of the ideological goals of present day America.

BRAT. Wow. That's a real press conference kind of prepared answer there.

MISSY. It was kind of a press conference kind of question.

BRAT. Yeah. You're right.

(A long pause. THEY look out at the party)

BRAT. So, what are you going to do next?

MISSY. I don't know ... I've run out of my family's home movies. Maybe I could talk about other people's families home movies. Or get my family to recreate exciting moments from my childhood. Or get actors to play my family or. Something. I'll do something.

BRAT. Cool. (*Long pause.*) A retrospective, huh? This must make you real happy.

MISSY. Happiness? Please. I do what I do.

BRAT. Right.

MISSY. You know what I mean?

BRAT. Exactly.

MISSY. Yeah?

BRAT. It's kind of like me and theater.

MISSY. How so?

BRAT. I like theater that has some, you know, bite in it. Which is how come I like your Bertolt Brecht.

(Throughout the play, BRAT uses the German pronunciation—Bear-tolt Bresht—everyone else uses the American.)

MISSY. Yes, I heard that.

BRAT. Well after I did Brecht for the first time, I really felt that I found, you know, something to sink my teeth into. And I knew I eventually wanted to do every play the guy wrote. I mean I do other things, c'mon, I'm an actor, I'll do anything. But Brecht ... For Brecht ... I would do Brecht for cab fare. No lie.

MISSY. How long have you been doing *Breshhhhhht?*

BRAT. Since Our Lady of Perpetual Sorrow.

MISSY. I don't know that play.

BRAT. It's a Catholic high school in New Jersey.

MISSY. Oh.

BRAT. It's where I went. I had one of those groovy nuns. With the short skirts, and the handcrafted crucifixes and the easy-care feminist hair.

MISSY. I loved them. I mean, I'm not Catholic or anything, but—

BRAT. Sister Marsha was her name, and she was real forward thinking and for junior class play, we did *Die Dreigroschenoper.*

MISSY. *Threepenny Opera* for those of us who aren't entirely pretentious.

BRAT. Very good. My first Brecht. I played Pirate Jenny.

MISSY. Isn't that a—

BRAT. It's a woman's role.

MISSY. Oh, you went to an all-boys school?

BRAT. No, Sister Marsha had a concept. Anyways, I had this one line in the *Second Threepenny Finale* where I would run to the front of the stage and shout, "Man will always thrive, because he will always step on the face of his own human kindness."

MISSY. See? Now, we did *Paint Your Wagon.*

BRAT. And I decided at that moment that that was the coolest feeling I ever felt. I was saying something socially relevant and I was being very intellectual on account of I was using what they call "Brechtian alienation." Not letting emotions interfere. Just pure thought. And, you know, I figured this is how I wanted to express myself artistically speaking. And so I really like doing Brecht and I audition for every Brecht play that comes down the pike.

MISSY. Oh yeah?

BRAT. I been very lucky.

MISSY. Great.

BRAT. Done about everything. Even *Die Lehrstuke.* And nobody does them.

MISSY. Oh. Well. Yeah.

BRAT. So, I've done just about everything. But I still feel ...

MISSY. (*Knowing what he means.*) Yes.

BRAT. Which is how come I said what you must feel about your work is what I feel about me and Brecht.

MISSY. Right.

BRAT. I done a lot.

MISSY. Right.

BRAT. Right. But I still feel—

MISSY. Exactly.

BRAT. But if I wanted more that would be—

MISSY. Greedy.

BRAT. Too aggressive or—
MISSY. Greed. Like Donald Trump greed. Or Erich—
BRAT & MISSY. Von Stroheim *Greed.*
MISSY. Yeah.
BRAT. Or something.
MISSY. Exactly.
BRAT. Right?
MISSY. Yeah.
BRAT. But there has to be more.
MISSY. Must be.
BRAT. But you know?
MISSY. Exactly.
BRAT. Yes.
MISSY. Well.
BRAT. Yes. Well. What can you do?
MISSY. What can you do?

(Long pause. THEY look out at the party.)

BRAT. This is a great thing this retrospective thing. *(Pause.)* Hm.
    MISSY. What?
    BRAT. Nothing.
    MISSY. No, what?
    BRAT. Just. Stupid. There's this line. That keeps rolling over in my head.
    MISSY. What?
    BRAT. A lot anymore. Silly.
    MISSY. Tell me.
    BRAT. It's stupid. It goes—uhm, "Let me tell you something and don't you ever forget it. Success is nothing without someone you love to share it with."

MISSY. Jesus. What's that from?

BRAT. *Mahog—*

MISSY *Mahogany.* Of course Brecht. *The Rise and Fall of the City of Mahogany.*

BRAT. No. *Mahogany.* The old Diana Ross movie.

MISSY Oh.

BRAT. Billy Dee Williams says it.

MISSY. Quite the line.

BRAT. Yeah. It's in the scene where she's the high fashion model in Rome and he's a failed politician visiting Rome and they come back from the party where she poured candle wax on herself and he got weirded out by Anthony Perkins and how come your eyes are wet?

MISSY. Nothing.

BRAT. And she says she's going to be a bigger success than he can ever see and are you allergic to something?

MISSY. No just uhm—How's that—"Success is nothing—"

BRAT. No. "Let me tell you something and don't you ever—"Are you O.K.?

MISSY. Yes.

BRAT. Hey. (*HE kisses her.*) You're too hard on yourself.

(*Kisses her again, lightly. HE realizes he likes it. THEY have a long passionate kiss. When it is over THEY just stare at one another.*)

MISSY. What was that about?

BRAT. I am very whoa here.

MISSY. Excuse me.

BRAT. That was—

MISSY. Young man, please remember your current preference. Spaz is —
BRAT. Right. I'll go talk to Spaz. Sorry.
MISSY. Don't. Let's just forget it.
BRAT. Sorry.

(HE runs off. MISSY stands alone for a moment. A look of deep consternation on HER face. Suddenly SHE laughs.)

MISSY. *Mahogany.*

(As SHE exits, SHE passes the photograph. Without looking, SHE flicks her glass and splashes the white wine on the oversized image of HER face.)

Scene 7

Telephones. Missy's bedroom. SUIT at an airport pay phone.
After the PHONE rings a number of times, MISSY runs in and grabs it. It is cordless.

MISSY. Hello?
SUIT. *(Into phone disguising his voice.)* Hello, ma'am, what do you use for your best sex?
MISSY. Is this Time-Life Books again?
SUIT. *(Regular voice.)* No, it's Suit.
MISSY. Oh, hi Suit. I thought it was someone trying to sell me those home repair and improvement books.

SUIT. You tramp.

MISSY. Talk dirty to me, why don't you?

SUIT. So listen, crazy lady, I'm in Los Angeles. At the airport. I'm at a pay phone. Let me give you my number in case we get disconnected. Area code 213. (*SHE jots it down.*) Number is 213-555-6020. Got it?

MISSY. Got it.

SUIT. O.K., Well, I've got my Filofax out here and I'm just trying to figure out when I can have my way with you.

MISSY. This week?

SUIT. Yes.

MISSY. Let me see.

SUIT. You got your Filofax out?

MISSY. Please. I've got a wall calendar.

SUIT. You put our appointments on a wall calendar?

MISSY. Nobody says anything, except when Spaz comes to visit he clutches it to his chest and sings, *Calendar Girl,* but —

SUIT. What a character. Ready?

MISSY. Sure.

SUIT. Tuesday?

MISSY. The 14th?

SUIT. Right. Afternoon?

MISSY. That's cool.

SUIT. And dinner?

MISSY. Great.

SUIT. And one week from Friday is dinner—

MISSY & SUIT. And the Joyce with Spaz and Brat.

SUIT. Now that Saturday—

MISSY. I can't. I have to give a lecture.

SUIT. Ahhhhh. Because that Saturday I was going to leave my wife for you.

MISSY. Yeah right.

SUIT. You don't believe me?

MISSY. Suit, please, it's your ploy.

SUIT. Hey?

MISSY. What?

SUIT. You wanna marry me?

MISSY. Suit, what are you possibly thinking? If you marry me, can you even conceive of what your company would do? And what would your friends do with my friends? How are they going to deal with Spaz and—

SUIT. So we could have parties without—

MISSY. Without Spaz? I'm sorry, I don't work that way. You want me, you get me and like all of what I am.

SUIT. And Spaz is you?

MISSY. No, but I am Spaz's friend. Look. O.K. I'm impressed that you had the nerve to use this ploy. It's very dangerous. And I appreciate the effort. But ... it's not possible. So don't whatever—bring it up again.

SUIT. O.K.

MISSY. I'm interested enough.

SUIT. O.K.

MISSY. O.K.

SUIT. Tuesday?

MISSY. Tuesday. Bye.

SUIT. Bye. (*HE hangs up.*)

(*MISSY hangs up slowly. Thinks for a moment, then suddenly picks up the scrap paper with Suit's number on it. SHE picks up the phone and pushes three*

*numbers. Then stops. SHE hangs up the phone. A
moment, then—)*

MISSY. (*Casually.*) I am not a well woman.

Scene 8

A restaurant.

SUIT. (*Making his way to a table with SPAZ, BRAT
and MISSY.*) Sorry I'm late.
SPAZ. You're late!!
SUIT. Just got back. Missy, I've been trying to call
you, there's something I have to tell you.
SPAZ. Sit down, Suit. No one has anything to tell
anyone before me. I have news.
SUIT. It's about—
SPAZ. Suit, perch. And have some champagne.
SUIT. Champagne? Why are we having champagne?
MISSY. What is with the champagne?
SPAZ. I ... just got ... B.A.M.
MISSY. Excuse me, hello? Brooklyn Academy Of
Music?
BRAT. Great, huh?
MISSY. The big, beautiful high point of performance
art.
SUIT. Congratulations.
MISSY. Spaz, you're performing again. I'm fully proud
of you.

SPAZ. Not performing, catering. I got the B.A.M. opening night party. I just got off the phone with ... Bianca Jag—

BRAT. Bianca Jagger!!

SPAZ. Bianca fucking Jagger. Could you possibly die?

SUIT. You're really taking off.

BRAT. Oh, yeah. He's getting orders left and right now.

SPAZ. And it's all because I was getting ready to give it all up.

MISSY. What?

SPAZ. I was in this bright indigo funk about choosing catering. And I was seriously contemplating just but chucking the whole thing. Considering getting back on all fours and grunting in the chorus for Meredith Monk. And I had to do this God forsaken dinner party for this tub o' lard trendy hostess. So I decided to just blow it off. She had requested fish. So I made her a tuna casserole and prayed to be blacklisted.

MISSY. A tuna casserole?

SPAZ. With a crust made of potato chips.

BRAT. Potato chips!

SPAZ. I thought for sure she would just freak. Have some more champagne. Well, she called after the party, turns out she just adored the casserole. They thought it was ironic. So far this week, I've made macaroni and cheese, meatloaf and ham spread for the richest and most influential people in America.

MISSY. Oh my God Spaz, you're a Post-Modern caterer.

SPAZ. So for B.A.M., do you think I should make creamed chipped beef?

MISSY. Nah, just stop off at a White Castle.

SPAZ. More champagne!!

SUIT. Well, I've got something else to celebrate with champagne.

BRAT. What?

SUIT. I have an announcement.

SPAZ. Suit, I love your suit.

BRAT. Shhhhh. Suit has an announcement.

SUIT. This is something that Missy and I have been talking about.

MISSY. Uh—oh.

SUIT. And we both thought that I would never have the nerve to do it.

SPAZ. You're going to loosen your tie?

SUIT. And now I've done it.

MISSY. Suit, you didn't.

SUIT. I did.

MISSY. Goddamn you.

SUIT. What?

MISSY. How like fucking dare you?

SUIT. What is your case?

MISSY. You just like—boom—make this decision without even so much as like a discussion with me.

SUIT. Miss, I—

MISSY. How could you—

SUIT. Missy, I didn't.

MISSY. What?

SUIT. I didn't.

MISSY. Oh.

SUIT. That's not my announcement.

MISSY. I just uhm—Oh God I'm like—You've just been talking about it lately and I—I guess I've become kind of nervous and—

SPAZ. This is the second most embarrassing situation I've ever been in, in my life.

BRAT. What was the first?

SPAZ. It involved a neighbor's dog.

BRAT. I've heard enough.

SUIT. Actually what I was announcing kind of concerns you guys. We, Missy and I, have been talking about some time when my wife and daughter are out of town that we would go utilize the summer house. Upstate. And invite you guys up too. So the four of us could have a weekend out of the city.

SPAZ. That would be great! When?

SUIT. One weekend from now.

SPAZ. A weekend in the country, pack my quiver and bow.

BRAT. Way cool.

SPAZ. Just us four.

SUIT. Four friends.

MISSY. Double dating. Sorry I like lost it earlier.

SUIT. It's O.K.

MISSY. Just made a big, beautiful embarrassment of myself.

SPAZ. Like that's never happened before. More champagne.

MISSY. I have too much champagne.

SPAZ. There's no such thing as too much champagne.

BRAT. You're so eighties.

SPAZ. I'll have you know, I'm timeless.

MISSY. So what are we eating?

BRAT. Appetizers!

SPAZ. Appetize or die.

SUIT. Actually, I won't be eating.

MISSY. What?

SUIT. I have to split. Leave.

MISSY. Oh. O.K. Well. This is real ...

SUIT. I'm sorry to just spring this on you. Well, it's just lousy timing night here. And I—I thought I would be free but Jan is still in town and—So, uhm—Spaz, Brat? See you in two weekends.

BRAT. Great.

SUIT. Bye.

SPAZ. Country living. I'm ordering things from Talbot's first thing tomorrow.

SUIT. I'm sorry about tonight.

MISSY. I wish you'd told me.

SUIT. I just got back into town an hour ago. I didn't know till I called in to play back my messages and she picked up. I was on the way here. I tried to call—

MISSY. Just a ticket goes to waste tonight.

SUIT. Do you want money?

MISSY. That's not the point.

SUIT. Well what the fuck is the point?!!

SPAZ. Suit, please. Lower your voice. The waiters are dishing.

SUIT. Right. O.K., I'll call you. Bye.

MISSY. Take care, Suit.

SUIT. Bye.

MISSY. Take some big, beautiful care.

SUIT. O.K.

MISSY. Take large care, will ya?

SUIT. You're mad at me.

MISSY. Just take some economy-sized care.

SUIT. Shit. (*HE exits.*)

SPAZ. Wow. All the wordplay. You must be pissed.

MISSY. I'm pissed.

SPAZ. Pissy Missy. How come?

MISSY. Because he doesn't want to marry me.

SPAZ. Do you want to marry him?

MISSY. No, but I'd like him to want to marry me.

SPAZ. Why?

MISSY. I don't know.

SPAZ. Missy, this is Spaz. You can lie to yourself but not me.

MISSY. Lust. I would like to have someone around all the time to make the sex with. Let's order an appetizer.

SPAZ. Well if that's the case—

BRAT. Spaz, no.

SPAZ. I think I have the answer.

BRAT. Spaz, this is not the opportunity.

SPAZ. This is a golden opportunity.

MISSY. What's going on?

SPAZ. Well if you need to just have the sex, and Suit is not available, you should just have the proverbial bounce.

MISSY. Yeah, but—

BRAT. Not now.

SPAZ. With Brat.

BRAT. Oh God.

MISSY. You're kidding. Are you offering—

SUIT. Well ... Brat's been having hetero-urges lately, and ... I would feel much better if he slept with someone with a sense of style. And he likes you and you said he was an institution and well let's just kill two birds with one stone.

MISSY. This is an unbelievable offer.

SPAZ. Call before midnight tonight.

MISSY. I'll have to get back to you later.

SPAZ. Well, so far I've had a comeback, you're not getting married, your lover has stood you up, and we're arranging a sexual tryst. And we haven't even ordered appetizers yet.

Scene 9

Later.

MISSY. Yeah. Sure. Why not?

Scene 10

SUIT and MISSY in Missy's bedroom, BRAT and SPAZ in Spaz's kitchen.

SPAZ. (*To BRAT, who has just entered his kitchen.*) Hey.

SUIT. (*In Missy's bed, to MISSY who has just entered.*) Hello.

BRAT. Hey, Spaz.

MISSY. Suit, what are you doing here?

SPAZ. How did things go?

SUIT. Just got back from Canada. Let myself in.

SPAZ. How was your "date"?

SUIT. How's life without me?

BRAT & MISSY. O.K.

SUIT. Are you mad that I'm here?

SPAZ. Sorry I put you up to it?

MISSY & BRAT. No.

BRAT. It was—

MISSY. I'm—

MISSY & BRAT. Fine.

SUIT & SPAZ. Great.

SPAZ. So, how was she?

BRAT. That's a pig thing to say.

SPAZ. I'm trying to be heterosexual.

BRAT. It's not working.

SPAZ. All right, Mac, how was your lay?

BRAT. It was very good.

SPAZ Very good? Beans? Please spill.

BRAT. I'm not going to do that. That wouldn't be very—

SPAZ. Gentlemanly?

BRAT. Well, yeah.

SPAZ. Oh, Brat, you're just too Merchant Ivory for words.

MISSY. What did you do?

BRAT. O.K., O.K., we had drinks—

SUIT. Made more money.

BRAT. We went to my place, we had wine,

SUIT. Lots of money.

BRAT. We laid on the floor, we talked about dumb stuff we had in common—you know, we both know all the words to *Desderada*? We laughed a lot.

MISSY. (*To herself smiling.*) "Strive to be happy. You are a child of the universe ..."

SUIT. What?

MISSY. Nothing.

BRAT. We made lo—had sex, we showered, she left.

MISSY. Daydreaming. Sorry.

SPAZ. "We made lo—had sex"? Your Freudian slip is showing.

BRAT. Spaz, calm down. I came back to you. I'm here, aren't I?

SPAZ. Right, right, right. Oh God. You and your women.

MISSY. Suit?

SUIT. Yeah?

MISSY. I want to be totally honest about this. There's something I have to tell you.

SUIT. Is it painful?

MISSY. Might be.

SUIT. So don't be totally honest.

MISSY. Suit, I had sex with someone besides you or myself.

SUIT. Oh.

MISSY. Do you want to know who?

SUIT. Only if it's important.

MISSY. Well, I guess if you're not interested, then it's not important.

SUIT. O.K.

MISSY. So I won't tell you. (*A pause.*) It was Brat.

SUIT. Brat?!

SPAZ. Brat?

BRAT. What?

SPAZ. How was it?

SUIT. How could you?
BRAT. What?
SPAZ. Having sex with her?
SUIT. Brat? I don't believe you.
BRAT. It was good.
MISSY. I had desire.
MISSY & BRAT. What do you want from me?
SUIT. What made you want him?
MISSY. He was available.
SPAZ. I want to know.
MISSY. And cute.
SPAZ. What's it like having sex with a woman?
SUIT. Is that safe?
MISSY. Of course.
BRAT. It's—I don't know.
MISSY. Everything was very up and up.
BRAT. You want to know, try it.
SUIT. Do you have a crush on him?
SPAZ. No thanks. But you enjoyed?
MISSY & BRAT. It was convenient sex.
BRAT. What's not to enjoy?
SUIT. What about Spaz?
BRAT. You arranged it.
MISSY. He arranged it.
SPAZ. I know, I know.
SUIT. Jesus. Artists.
SPAZ. I just worry.
MISSY & BRAT. What does that mean?
SPAZ. Have you fallen in love?
SUIT. Have you fallen in love?

MISSY.	BRAT.
Oh, God, no. There's no way I'm going to muck up not only my career but every relationship I have in the world. I like things the way they are now, thank you very much	No, not at all, it doesn't interest me to pursue a lovey-dovey thing even with a woman. Things are good as is.

MISSY. No.

BRAT. Not at all.

SPAZ. O.K.

SUIT. Cool.

SPAZ. That's cool.

SUIT. As long as it's not going to be awkward.

SPAZ. Oh. Suit called.

SUIT. I called Spaz.

SPAZ. We're going upstate this weekend.

SUIT. This is the weekend we're going upstate.

SPAZ. Turns out I'm doing a party in Albany.

SUIT. Spaz has a party in Albany.

SPAZ & SUIT. So, I'll meet him in Hudson.

SUIT. You'll have to pick up Brat.

SPAZ. Missy will pick you up.

SUIT & SPAZ. There's a 7:10 train from Grand Central.

SUIT. You'll get off at Hudson.

SPAZ. Take the Amtrak to Hudson.

BRAT. Great.

SUIT. O.K.?

SPAZ. Super.

MISSY. Sure.

SPAZ. Come to bed.

SUIT. Come to bed.

(A long pause. BRAT and MISSY just stare forward into space.)

MISSY. Yeah.
BRAT. Sure.

Scene 11

The roof of Brat's building.

MISSY. Hey.
BRAT. Hey hey.
MISSY. I saw your note on your door saying you were up sunbathing. Is it safe up here?
BRAT. Thought I'd catch some color before I exposed my big, beautiful whiteness to the wilderness.
MISSY. Seriously.
BRAT. You're early.
MISSY. Yeah well, I thought I'd ... I got done early so ... what are you listening to?
BRAT. Billie Holiday.
MISSY. Great. She's great.
BRAT. The best.
MISSY. Great, uhm—
BRAT. Phrasing?
MISSY. Right. And you can hear the tragedy in her voice.

BRAT. Do you think it's tragedy? I thought it sounded more like she was this very elegant lady and underneath it all she was kind of this frightened child. That's what I hear in her voice.

MISSY. Yeah?

BRAT. And I want to protect her.

MISSY. I think you're a little late.

BRAT. My timing bites.

MISSY. Brat?

BRAT. Yeah?

MISSY. How come your nickname is Brat?

BRAT. My folks.

MISSY. Oh.

BRAT. I think I cried out loud one time too many because I wanted more of something. And I already had a grandfather and three uncles named, "Tony" so it was getting confusing, so—

MISSY. So.

BRAT. So.

MISSY. Uhm, something's up.

BRAT. What's up?

MISSY. Something.

BRAT. Where?

MISSY. Here.

BRAT. What do you mean?

MISSY. I've been feeling something like up since we slept together.

BRAT. Embarrassment?

MISSY. Well, that, yeah. And something kind of else.

BRAT. What?

MISSY. Well, you know—O.K., you now have to promise not to just like burst out into gales of hysterical laughter here or say something like snarly or derisive because as solid as I no doubt appear to you, I am like unspeakably wobbly and just a big tower of whatever.

BRAT. Jello.

MISSY. Right.

BRAT. What?

MISSY. I think possibly, vaguely, in a roundabout way, I sort of maybe ... like love you.

BRAT. I've been feeling those feelings too, I feel.

MISSY. And I know it's real silly and real just awkward, but that is going—excuse me, but did you just—

BRAT. Like love. Like falling. Is that the right expression?

MISSY. Oh, God, are you sure?

BRAT. It's happened before and I swore it wouldn't happen again but—you know—hello—here it is.

MISSY. And not just sexual infatuation.

BRAT. Nah, I've done that.

MISSY. Me too.

BRAT. No ... like love ... like—

MISSY. It's like death. Like almost death. Like what you feel on an amusement park ride or in near-miss car accidents. Like death-defying.

BRAT. Oh shit.

MISSY. "Oh shit," what?

BRAT. Love. We are, you know, falling here.

MISSY. What should we do?

BRAT. Kiss, I guess.

MISSY. But I—

BRAT. Shhhh. Let's listen to Billie. And kiss some.

MISSY. No. No. Stop it. I am not going to get, uhm, taken in by a romantic setting and a cute guy and music from the forties being sung by some singer who sounds like she's been roused from a deep sleep.

BRAT. Why do you fight this?

MISSY. Because it's goofy. It's not me. It's not at all me. It's—

BRAT. Are you afraid?

MISSY. I take affront to your tone here.

BRAT. Are you?

MISSY. Of course I'm afraid!! Aren't you?

BRAT. Yeah. That's how I know it's probably the right thing to do.

MISSY. You're really ...

BRAT. What?

MISSY. Getting on my nerves.

BRAT. But you're falling in love with me.

MISSY. I don't want this. Go away.

BRAT. Do you want me to go away?

MISSY. (*Beginning to cry.*) No.

BRAT. You know what Brecht says.

MISSY. I hate Brecht.

BRAT. I love Brecht.

MISSY. I hate you.

BRAT. I love you.

MISSY. I love you too. But I hate you. It's like I was very happy sitting by the side of the pool dangling my feet in the water, but you have gone and pushed me in. Right in the middle of the adult swim. And I hate you for it.

BRAT. How do you feel about Brecht?

MISSY. I hate Brecht! And I hate people who say Breshhhht!

BRAT. How do you feel about Billie Holiday?

MISSY. Oh. Who cares!!!

BRAT. Do you like this song? This is called, "Easy Living."

MISSY And I—(*HE kisses her.*) I hate—

(*THEY kiss.*)

MISSY. I love—

(*THEY kiss. SHE places her head on his shoulder. THEY begin to dance. HE even sings a little bit. The part about "being a fool but it's fun."*)

MISSY. Brat?
BRAT. Still here.
MISSY. I'm falling in love.
BRAT. That's nice.
MISSY. It's very bourgeois of me, isn't it?
BRAT. Yes.
MISSY. Very suburbia.
BRAT. I'm so embarrassed for you.

(*THEY kiss.*)

Scene 12

Amtrak Station Hudson, N.Y.

SPAZ. I just spoke to the porter and he said there was no one who fit their description on the train.
SUIT. And everybody—

SPAZ. And everybody who's getting off has gotten off.
SUIT. Shit.
SPAZ. So they missed the train.
SUIT. Well, that was a miscalculation. Scheduling for the last train of the day.
SPAZ. No later trains?
SUIT. Fuck!
SPAZ. No later trains.
SUIT. Perhaps they've left a message at the house.
SPAZ. Right. We should check the machine from here.
SUIT. Yes. I guess.
SPAZ. Are there trains tomorrow?
SUIT. Eight o'clock in the morning.
SPAZ. What could have held them up?
SUIT. I don't know. What could have held them up?

(After a moment, THEY look at one another. THEY know. We hear Billie singing about being a fool again ...)

End of Act I

Scene 1

Suit's too beautiful Columbia County country house.
SUIT enters and looks at Spaz. SPAZ is stretched out on
the sofa in the stylishly rustic house. Wearing a Details
view of western apparel, SPAZ is reading a copy of
"Alice in Wonderland." A quilt is over his legs.

SUIT. How do you feel?

SPAZ. Trapped in a Ralph Lauren ad.

SUIT. No, I mean physically.

SPAZ. Better.

SUIT. I can't believe you never went fishing before.

SPAZ. Only for compliments.

SUIT. You did pretty well. Until you threw up.

SPAZ. I'm just not used to being in a rocking boat
with dying flapping things. That early.

SUIT. You've got to get up at sunrise to get the best
fish. I also can't believe you can't swim. You should learn
to swim.

SPAZ. A non-swimmer is what I am, no use changing.

SUIT. Sorry if that life jacket was uncomfortable.

SPAZ. I'm intrigued to wear anything called a Mae
West.

SUIT. Sorry you fell in the lake.

SPAZ. Suit?

SUIT. Yeah?

SPAZ. I just want you to know. I'm being a very good
guest.

SUIT. Sure. You're doing fine.

SPAZ. No, I don't think you understand. It's been raining a lot. And there isn't anything to do. I'm being a very, very good guest.

SUIT. See, I didn't count on the rain.

SPAZ. And when it wasn't raining, I went on the lake. And the lake made me very sick. And then I fell in the lake. And you fished me out. With an oar.

SUIT. Right.

SPAZ. I'm being a great guest.

SUIT. Maybe it will stop raining. And they won't call off the Shaker crafts fair. I wish I'd planned more activities. I just counted on us being a foursome and—I'm sorry all we have for activities are Lizbeth's things.

SPAZ. Your daughter has excellent taste in literature. I've been meaning to reread this Lewis Carroll piece for years.

SUIT. How is it?

SPAZ. Gripping. I'm on chapter five

SUIT. So would you like to do something?

SPAZ. Sure.

SUIT. You want to play a game or something?

SPAZ. Sure. Let's play a game.

SUIT. "Candyland" or "Go Fish"?

SPAZ. "Candyland."

(SUIT sets up the board.)

SPAZ. Gosh. I love board games.

SUIT. That doesn't sound very earnest.

SPAZ. I'm not Earnest in the country. I'm Jack.

SUIT. *(Not getting it.)* Huh?

SPAZ. Never mind.

SUIT. I feel that I should mention that I do feel comfortable right now.

SPAZ. Why did you feel you had to mention that?

SUIT. Well, I wanted you to know it. And I wanted to make sure—well, I don't usually feel comfortable—I mean I never feel entirely comfortable with gay men. I always think that they're—

SPAZ. Coming on to you?

SUIT. Laughing at me. Like I'm not getting their jokes. If I was being totally ignorant you wouldn't laugh behind my back would you?

SPAZ. No, I would laugh right to your face.

SUIT. Thanks. It's not like I dislike gay people or anything.

SPAZ. May we change the subject?

SUIT. I'm sorry you people don't have equal rights.

SPAZ. Oh well. That's all right.

SUIT. Wonder why that is?

SPAZ. Let's play the game.

SUIT. O.K. You start. And stay out of the molasses swamp.

(THEY begin to play.)

SUIT. So ... why do you think Missy and Brat missed the train?

SPAZ. I don't know.

SUIT. Do you think ... They'll really ... probably come up today.

SPAZ. Don't know. Maybe.

SUIT. You're very calm about all this.

SPAZ. Yes well. It's a new thing I'm working with. It's called not caring.

SUIT. You don't care?

SPAZ. No. Not really. Well, I do care, but when things happen and I, you know—

SUIT. Care?

SPAZ. Yeah. I ... distract myself. I just list the presidents of the United States. Alphabetically. And ... I don't care.

(Pause.)

SUIT. So, do you think Missy and Brat did ... get it on last night?

SPAZ. Hmmmm.

SUIT. What?

SPAZ. I'm thinking.

SUIT. What?

SPAZ. The last time I heard the expression "Get it on." Probably the last time I played "Candyland."

SUIT. It's been a while since you played hasn't it?

SPAZ. Does it show?

SUIT. You're headed for the molasses swamp.

SPAZ. Straight men and sports. I'm just not prepared.

SUIT. I'm used to playing with Lizbeth.

SPAZ. How is she to play with?

SUIT. She cheats.

(SPAZ smiles.)

SUIT. You're thinking "Like father, like daughter" right?

SPAZ. Am I that obvious?

SUIT. Pretty much.

SPAZ. Thank you. Lose one turn.

SUIT. I don't really like it when she cheats. You know? She—uhm ... I would like her to be above that. Not like— I don't mean to make it sound like I want her to be better than me. I mean my life is fine. Secure. I'm proud of my solidness. Not that I'm insensitive to others when they're unsolid. I mean, I've had my moments of fragility, I guess. Back in my—God, must have been sophomore year of college—Jesus, I was out there. Very erratic. Met this girl, her name was ... don't even remember. Beautiful. Looked like Cheryl Tiegs. I was a mess. Just, as I said, out there. Couldn't think of anything but being with her and drinking thick red wine and making love and writing awful poems that rhymed and ... what was her name? My grades were in the basement. My dad—oh God—embarrassing memory— My dad had to come down and give me one of those your-mother-and-I lectures. "Your mother and I." (*HE laughs.*) God. I used to get those speeches semi-annually like reports. But this time my old man seemed—I don't know—pretty fragile himself. Couldn't look me in the eye. And Dad was big on eye contact. I could make eye contact before I could walk. So I broke up with the girl whose name I can't remember but who apparently was so important at the time. What can I tell you? I'm not one of those people who carry on like a French singer, right? "Life is to be lived on the edge, ho ho."

SPAZ. Hate them.

(SUIT stops playing, SPAZ continues.)

SUIT. Just doesn't appeal to me. I don't really think life needs to be so fragile. Just ... keep it fine. Let's calm down and make money and let that be that. Not that I'm only a capitalist. I give back. I give back to the world. I give to the homeless and I give to cure Aids and I give to the ... the ...

SPAZ. The what?

SUIT. The other one.

(THEY BOTH think for a moment, then.)

SPAZ. The environment.

SUIT. Right. The environment. So that Lizbeth can have things ... solid. With a good foundation. *(Pause.)* And other people, too. *(Pause.)* Solid and grounded and secure and *(Pause. HE smiles.)* Loretta. Loretta something. *(Pause. The smile fades.)* And safe and fine.

(Pause. THEY BOTH stare at the game board for awhile.)

SPAZ. Why are we staring at the board?

SUIT. The game is over.

SPAZ. Who won?

SUIT. Me.

SPAZ. When did you beat me?

SUIT. Back when I said I wasn't a French singer.

SPAZ. *(Looks as if HE is going to go berserk, but suddenly closes his eyes and—)* Adams, Adams, Arthur, Buchanan, Carter, Cleveland, Coolidge, Eisenhower, Fillmore, Garfield—

(A CAR is heard.)

SUIT. What's that?

SPAZ. What's that noise?

SUIT. Sounds like a car.

SPAZ. Who is it?

SUIT. I don't know.

SPAZ. I don't care, I just hope they have backgammon. I hope they have literature. I hope they have pornography.

SUIT. It's a blue four-door.

SPAZ. It's Missy!

SUIT. Alone.

SPAZ. Where's Brat?

SUIT. She's alone.

SPAZ. What is going on?

MISSY. (*Entering.*) Hi. I found you. I can't believe I found you. Some like town cracker like *Twin* like fucking *Peaks* gave me directions. I think I broke a Toyota.

SUIT. Where were you last night?

MISSY. I rented it and broke it.

SPAZ. Where's Brat?

MISSY. Great place, Suit. It looks like Kennebunkport on ecstacy.

SPAZ. *Bush!* Adams, Adams, Arthur, Buchanan, *Bush.*

SUIT. Spaz!

SPAZ. I forgot him. And he's so popular.

SUIT. Spaz, be serious.

SPAZ. O.K., where's Brat?

MISSY. Brat is back in the city. Could one of you look at my broken car? Nice furniture. Anything left at the Ethan Allen's?

SPAZ. Back in the city?

SUIT. You O.K.?

MISSY. I'm like frazzled and exhausted and—
SUIT. Would you like some tea? Hot milk?
SPAZ. Beer?
MISSY. It's eleven o'clock in the morning. Corona.

(SPAZ runs into the kitchen.)

SUIT. What's wrong?
MISSY. Everything, everything. Oh goddamn it, Suit. *(Breaks down.)*
SPAZ. *(Entering with beer.)* Don't cry, Missy, it's only a Toyota.
SUIT. I think it's something serious.
MISSY. Oh God.
SUIT. It's O.K., it's O.K.
MISSY. Oh Suit.
SUIT. Yes, Missy.
MISSY. Oh Suit ... you're not wearing a suit. You look very ... catalog.
SUIT. And you look upset.
MISSY. Oh shit. *(Takes a swig of beer.)* I hate drinking beer in the morning. *(SHE takes another swig.)* Look at you, Spaz. Does Ronald Reagan know you're wearing his ranch clothing?
SPAZ. Why isn't Brat coming up?
MISSY. He uhm—I kind of came up without him.
SPAZ. What?
MISSY. Why?
SPAZ. Did you two fight?
MISSY. Oh God, I don't know. It's all too much. I'm like an emotional cripple here, I think I broke a rented car, my nerves are like "later." I just—

SPAZ. Calm down, calm down.

SUIT. Right, calm down. Spaz and I will just ask questions, and you answer.

MISSY. Easy questions.

SPAZ. O.K., easy questions. Why a blue four-door?

MISSY. That's all they had.

SUIT. What happened with Brat?

MISSY. Oh God. O.K., here goes. Last night Brat and I made love.

SPAZ. So that's why you're late!

SUIT. You could have had sex with me last night.

SPAZ. You know, that makes twice in the last week that you've had sex with my sex partner. There is such thing as bad taste.

MISSY. Not had sex, made love.

SPAZ. What?

MISSY. Brat and I—like stupid—have sort of fallen in love.

SUIT. What do you mean?

SPAZ. They're in love. Adams, Adams, Arthur—

SUIT. In love?

MISSY. Yes yes yes. Just don't get worked up. I took care of it, O.K.? I finished it.

SPAZ. How do you just finish it?

MISSY. O.K., from the top. Last night Brat and I made wild passionate love and really just defined love in our times. On the roof of his building.

SPAZ. How precarious.

MISSY. Then we went down to his apartment and we defined love again. We redefined love a number of times. And this morning, when I woke up next to someone that I truly loved, I felt joy. Happiness. Giddiness. And I sang. To myself. A song from the radio. I sang ... soft rock.

SPAZ. Repulsive.

MISSY. And I looked at my life and I felt this—I felt like this is like it. This is what I want ahead of me. To wake up next to someone I like love and do my work. So I got up to do some work and I—I couldn't. I had no interest in watching pictures of my early life and making disparaging comments. I wanted to do something else. Something more ... whatever ... I don't know, something else. Something with paint. And drawing. Something ... I wanted to do wet art. And I know that I could, but—For some like mysterious old reason I freaked. So I just—got dressed, got to National, got a rental, got on the Taconic.

SUIT. What are you saying?

SPAZ. She's saying she's come back to you.

MISSY. I'm ... back to you.

SUIT. Well, O K., Missy. You did the right thing.

SPAZ. You did the right thing. I personally would have waited for a two-door.

SUIT. So well now. Hey.

MISSY. Hey.

SUIT. I'm very—

MISSY. Happy.

SUIT. Whatever.

MISSY. O.K.

SPAZ. That Brat. I'll kill him.

SUIT. Well, O. K., Missy. So would you like a tour of the house?

MISSY. Yeah. Oh, but first, do either of you know anything about fixing rental cars? This car is doing a ping stopping thing.

SUIT. How bad is it?

MISSY. I think it might explode.

SUIT. I'll check it out. And when I get back, you'll get the grand tour. (*HE exits.*)

(An awkward pause between MISSY and SPAZ.)

MISSY. Well, you two ... you guys are getting along great. Away from it all.

SPAZ. Norman and I are coming to understand one another here on Golden Pond.

MISSY. You're having fun.

SPAZ. I'm a great guest. Just ask me.

MISSY. He's a good guy, Suit.

SPAZ. Very nice.

MISSY. He's not evil. There are other guys I could be in this situation with that would be so evil.

SPAZ. So insecure about your Brat decision that you need my approval?

MISSY. It's not like I chose Brat. Not like I went out of my way, I mean he's kind of a jerk ... and ... Oh, Spaz. I need a friend to talk to. About all of this. And you're the only friend I've got. But I can't talk to you because—

SPAZ. You're right, I can't talk to you.

MISSY. Not about this.

SPAZ. No. You know, now that his whole situation has come to pass, I'm beginning to realize more and more that something my dear old Aunt Adele always used to say is quite true. "Don't fuck in your own backyard."

MISSY. Your Aunt Adele sounds—

SPAZ. Oh. Total whore. Holiday Inn cocktail lounges.

MISSY. Tight knit dresses.

SPAZ. Bright red lips, Cleopatra make-up.

(THEY laugh, THEY hug. THEY fall onto the sofa. SPAZ on his back, MISSY on top of Spaz.)

MISSY. *(Feeling something against her.)* What's that?
SPAZ. My book.
MISSY. Oh.
SPAZ. Don't get your hopes up.

(THEY laugh.)

MISSY. *(Picking up book.)* "Alice in Wonderland." First time reading it?
SPAZ. Once as a child, when everything meant nothing. Once in art school, when I was—
MISSY. Wasted.
SPAZ. Exactly. So nothing meant everything. This is my first time as a grown up. Or whatever they call people like us. When everything means something. I'm on chapter five.
MISSY. *(Reading.)* "Advice From a Caterpillar."
SPAZ. Look at the Tenniel drawing.
MISSY. Ahhhhhh.
SPAZ. Look at Alice. The eyes. Looking up at the caterpillar on that mushroom. Look at her eyes. So open and scared but still full of whatever. What do kids have that give them that? And what do we lose? Choices are like made once and we just kind of follow them out.
MISSY. Alice has great eyes. She always did. So ... uhm ... would you like to read to me?

SPAZ. I would like to read to you. (*Reading.*) "Chapter Five. Advice From a Caterpillar. The Caterpillar and Alice looked at each other for some time in silence: at last the Caterpillar took the hookah out of it's mouth,

MISSY. Hookah? Do you have any—

SPAZ. No. (*Continuing to read.*) "and addressed her in a languid, sleepy voice. 'Who are you?' said the caterpillar. This was not an encouraging opening for a conversation. Alice replied rather shyly, 'I—I hardly know, sir, just at present—at least I know who I was when I got up this morning, but I think I must have been changed several times since then.' "

MISSY. Real Hayley Mills thing there for Alice. It works.

SPAZ. Thank you. (*Reading.*) " 'What do you mean by that?', said the caterpillar sternly, 'Explain yourself!' 'Well, perhaps you haven't found it so yet', said Alice, 'but when you have to turn into a chrysalis—and you will some day you know—and then after that into a butterfly, I should think you'll feel it a little queer, won't you?' 'Not a bit', said the caterpillar.' "

MISSY. " 'Not a bit', said the caterpillar."

SPAZ. Well, your feelings may be different—

SUIT. (*Reentering.*) Did anyone order a pizza?

MISSY. No.

SPAZ. Why do you ask?

SUIT. There's a jeep on the way up the hill.

SPAZ. Maybe it's going to another house.

SUIT. We're the only house on the hill.

MISSY. Oh my God.

SUIT. What?

SPAZ. Brat?

SUIT. He wouldn't.
MISSY. Did not my actions say, "no"?
SPAZ. He's an actor, he thinks "no" means "maybe."
SUIT. It's Brat.

(The sound of a JEEP.)

MISSY. What do we do?
SPAZ. Act casual.
SUIT. Confront him on the porch.
MISSY. Yes!
SUIT. Maybe I should beat him up or something.
SPAZ. Oh, please.
MISSY. You couldn't.
SUIT. I could try.
SPAZ. An activity! Is it too late to start a quilt?
MISSY. Play a game!
SUIT & SPAZ. No.
MISSY. Hide me! What the fu—
BRAT. (*Enters on THEM scampering around and then striking casual poses. A moment as HE takes it all in, then tries to make his presence known.*) Hey.
SPAZ. (*Looking up from book.*) Oh, hello.
SUIT. Hi.
MISSY. Hello.
BRAT. This must be the place.
MISSY. Uhm, Brat.
SPAZ. Brat.
SUIT. Brat.
BRAT. Missy, what is going on?
MISSY. You know very well what is going on.
BRAT. You just walked out on me.

MISSY. Wasn't that statement enough?

BRAT. I want to know how come.

MISSY. Why? Are you a glutton for punishment?

BRAT. Missy, goddamn it, I fucking love you.

SPAZ. Language.

SUIT. Hold it right there, fella.

BRAT. Suit, I don't want to have to fight you.

SUIT. O.K.

BRAT. Missy—I—

MISSY. How can you even say that you love me? After I left? You're a very superficial person.

BRAT. I know. Well, O.K. Initially when I woke up and you were gone, I never wanted to see you again. But the truth of it is that I can't get you out of my head. So indications are that I'm in love with you and we have to deal with this real quick.

MISSY. Love? You know, what is love? You come in here getting everyone upset throwing around this total Marvin Hamlisch of a word.

BRAT. That's not—

SUIT. Calm down, Brat.

MISSY. And what is that, right? I mean love? I'm not well. How many possible little variations do we just lump together with that label? You know the ancient Greeks had like seven words for different kinds of love. Love of like nature and shit. Love, like, what? Of self. Love of inanimate objects. Right now, this chair. I hardly know it. But I love it. So what is love? Love is an unknown chair.

SPAZ. Who is writing this shit?

BRAT. You know very well—

MISSY. How can you say—

BRAT. I'm talking love like that you would want to make a commitment with.

SPAZ. And speaking of commitment.

BRAT. Oh God. Spaz.

SPAZ. You just found the secret square.

BRAT. Do you know what's coming down here?

SPAZ. "Going down"? I put that somewhere with "get it on." Yes. I think I know what's coming down here, dude. But I think it would prove really eye-opening to have you tell me.

BRAT. O.K. Spaz, you have to understand something first. I care for you a lot. You are really one of the fine people around. But I don't love you and you don't love me. The two of us together wouldn't let love happen. So all we became was friends who ... you know. (*Awkwardly indicates sexual intercourse.*) Now, I have found someone who has taken my heart—upsetting visual, I know—and I'm going to do everything in my power to create a world with her. Now, I still want to be your friend. Without the ... you know. (*Awkwardly indicates sexual intercourse.*) And I'm sure she would too. Even though you two never ... you know. (*Awkwardly indicates sexual intercourse.*) But if you don't, I will respect that.

(*Pause.*)

SPAZ. I am not speaking to anyone for the next five minutes. (*HE exits through the main door and goes outside.*)

BRAT. Missy.

MISSY. Get away from me.

BRAT. Miss.

MISSY. Suit?

SUIT. Yes?

MISSY. Beat him up.

SUIT. He doesn't want to fight me.

MISSY. Why don't men resort to violence anymore?

BRAT. Missy, I—

MISSY. Love?

BRAT. Yes.

MISSY. Please.

BRAT. And you—

MISSY. Me?

BRAT. Yes.

MISSY. Love?

BRAT. Yes.

MISSY. Like Marvi—

BRAT. Like Marvin Hamlisch, Montevanni, 1001 Strings, yeah. Love.

MISSY. You?

BRAT. Yes.

MISSY. No.

BRAT. No?

MISSY. No, I don't love you.

BRAT. You don't love—

MISSY. I don't love anyone, so like—

BRAT. Do you love Suit?

SUIT. Brat, now come on!

BRAT. Do you?

MISSY. I—God—Now—What?

SUIT. Brat, this is really getting tasteless.

BRAT. Missy, do you love Suit?

MISSY. Well, God, I don't think—What does it prove?

BRAT. Does Suit love you?

MISSY. You're really not well about this.

BRAT. Suit, do you love Missy?

SUIT. None of your business.

BRAT. Missy, do you love Suit?

MISSY. It's not—all right—If you want to like put a real bright spotlight on it, no. Not really. No, I don't love Suit.

BRAT. And does Suit love you?

MISSY. I'm just—I don't think I—I don't know. Suit, do you—

SUIT. No

BRAT. See?

MISSY. *(To Suit.)* You didn't have to be so quick about it?

BRAT. What are you doing with your life? He doesn't love you and you don't love him. So, what is your life?

MISSY. Would—

SUIT. *(Looking out window.)* Oh God.

MISSY. You please. For me—

SUIT. Oh shit!

MISSY. As a favor.

SUIT. Guys.

MISSY. Do not even—

SUIT. Guys.

MISSY. Suit, please.

SUIT. Guys, when Spaz said before that he couldn't swim, was he for real?

BRAT. Yes.

SUIT. Oh shit.

MISSY. Not a stroke, why?

SUIT. He jumped in the lake.

BRAT. Spaz!

MISSY. Oh my God, get him!

SUIT. Shit!

BRAT. (*Removing his shoes.*) What the—(*HE runs off.*)

MISSY. (*Taking a life preserver off the wall.*) Save him. *(SHE exits.)*

(SUIT takes oar from the wall, then exits.)

Scene 2

The same. An hour later.

BRAT, wearing a white terry robe, is seated. His hair is wet. Four electronic beeps are heard. MISSY enters from the bedroom. Without making eye contact, SHE walks over and opens louvre door revealing the source of the beeps. A dryer. With sudden fury SHE hurls Brat's clothes from the dryer at Brat. Then, casually returns to the bedroom. BRAT picks up his clothes and gets dressed. In doing so, HE shows us the back of the robe, which is embroidered with the name of one of Wall Street's more prestigious firms. When HE is finished, MISSY reenters with a mug of tea and sits on the sofa. BRAT opens his mouth to speak to her.

MISSY. Save it.

BRAT. What?

MISSY. Just save it. Don't really want to hear it.

BRAT. I just want to know how Spaz is?

MISSY. Fat fucking lot you care.

(Pause.)

BRAT. Fat lot? Isn't that a British expression?

MISSY. I put fucking in it, now it's American.

BRAT. So what's with Spaz?

MISSY. He's fine.

BRAT. Is he?

MISSY. Just a little winded.

BRAT. Good. Is he up and around or—

MISSY. He's in bed.

BRAT. Poor guy.

MISSY. Propped up in bed. Surrounded by pillows. Looking like a Puerto Rican bride doll.

BRAT. So he's—

MISSY. He'll be fine.

BRAT. Missy—

MISSY. Brat, please.

BRAT. Please what?

MISSY. Just like leave. Please. Please leave, O.K.?

(Long pause.)

BRAT. So uhm ... I guess you're aware that I love you. I mean, has that hit you yet?

MISSY. Yes!!!

BRAT. How come you're so hostile?

MISSY. If I am hostile it is because you have the like serious gumption to think that I would give up my everything-I-have to like be your little chickie.

BRAT. I'm not asking you to give up what you have. When did I ask you to give up what you have?

MISSY. No, but if I take up with you, I probably won't be able to do what I do.

BRAT. Who said you can't still be an artist?

MISSY. I probably couldn't be the same kind of artist.

BRAT. So be a different kind of artist.

MISSY I have a reputation. I have a style. I have grants that I'm still working off.

BRAT. What? And you don't think I'll have to change my acting? You don't think I'll have to change my style of theatre if I have love in my heart? Brechtian alienation is like out the window. I'll probably want to do—(*With a shudder.*) Romantic Naturalism. But I'll put the same energy I put into changing my work into our love.

MISSY. Brat, I can't put the same energy into love that I put into a career. There's no guarantee that I'll get back what I put in. There is that guarantee with work.

BRAT. Life hasn't got any guarantees.

MISSY. Do you think this persistence is like even remotely endearing?

BRAT. Would you—

MISSY. O.K. What if I did just say, "O.K. I like love you" and let that influence and change my work, who's to say this like love would last? Who's to say that two weeks from now you're not going to get bored? Or get sick and get dead? And then I'll be alone. With this romantic outlook on life. And art that probably will not be popular. No. That's too intimidating.

BRAT. But who's to say we're not going to grow very old together? And stay in love? And eat cat food?

MISSY. Exactly, who's to say?

BRAT. Who's to say?

MISSY. There's no guarantee.

BRAT. Life hasn't got—

MISSY. Yes it does! If you make passionless choices there are all the guarantees you could hope for!!

SUIT. (*Enters.*) Would you two—

BRAT. And passion —

SUIT. Hey. Will you two keep your voices down. Spaz is not up to being disturbed.

MISSY. Oh, God. Is he still in bed?

SUIT. No, rooting through the closet, criticizing my wife's clothing.

BRAT. Missy—

SUIT. Brat, now come on. Get a hold of yourself. You're behaving like a spoiled child, Brat.

MISSY. Thank you.

SUIT. And what you're saying, Brat, is some of the most immature jibberish. I think it's time you started behaving and dealing with things in an adult manner.

MISSY. God, yes.

SUIT. Someone here should. Brat, get off of my property.

MISSY. (*Condescendingly.*) Thank you, Suit. That was very mature.

SUIT. Well what do you want from me?

MISSY. I don't want anything from anyone.

BRAT. That's a lie.

MISSY. Fuck you, that's a lie.

SUIT. Brat. It's time for you to leave.

BRAT. Yeah well ... What if I don't want to leave.

SUIT. I don't see that you have a say in the matter. This is my house, this is my girl.

MISSY. I'm now inventory, I'm not well.

SUIT. You know what I mean. I didn't mean for it to come out that way. You know what our relationship is.

BRAT. What is your relationship?

SUIT. That's between us.

BRAT. Missy, what is your relationship with Suit? We know it's not love, so what is it?

MISSY. It's—It's very—Suit, what is—

SUIT. It's safe.

MISSY. Yes, it's safe. (*To Brat.*) It's safe. O.K.?

BRAT. And what else?

MISSY. And?

SUIT. And great sex.

MISSY. (*To Brat.*) And monumental sex, O.K.?

BRAT. And?

MISSY. That's enough, isn't it?

BRAT. Do you feel that it's enough? (*A pause, then gently.*) And?

MISSY. And? (*To Suit.*) And?

SUIT. And that's it.

MISSY. And—Oh my God. (*SHE is devastated.*)

BRAT. Missy.

MISSY. Get away from me. You made me doubt myself. I'll never forgive you for that.

BRAT. You don't mean that.

MISSY. I'm staying with Suit. I don't want to feel this way.

BRAT. But you were unhappy before.

MISSY. Yes, I was unhappy. But I didn't feel like I feel now. Now I feel like a shipwreck!

BRAT. Missy, I—

MISSY. I can't talk to you. I'm staying. I'm staying with Suit. I'm going to stay.

(Long pause.)

BRAT. Well.

MISSY. Sorry.

BRAT. Well now.

MISSY. I'm sorry.

BRAT. Right.

MISSY. You'll be alone now. I feel awful about that.

BRAT. I learned a lot in the last twenty-four hours. I'd rather be alone than what I was. *(HE starts to exit, gets to the door and turns around. HE is about to say something.)*

MISSY. Brat, goodbye. I'm going to go on with my life the way it was.

(BRAT turns to exit.)

SPAZ. *(Offstage.)* You do and you're a butthead.

MISSY. Spaz!

SPAZ. *(Entering.)* I mean like a total butthead.

MISSY. I'm sorry. I didn't know you could hear us in the bedroom.

SPAZ. You can't. You really have to stand by the closet to hear anything.

MISSY. Well, what are you saying?

SPAZ. I'm saying if you stay with Suit, you deserve all the misery you'll get.

SUIT. Missy, don't listen to him he's not entirely sane, he's just attempted suicide.

SPAZ. Suicide? God, Suit, get judgmental, why don't you? Yes, I jumped in the lake, but not because I wanted to die. Hardly. I jumped because I was so fucking sick of my life that I wanted to do something drastic to change it. I saw the water, I knew I couldn't swim, I wanted to learn to swim. I was swimming.

SUIT. You were drowning.

SPAZ. Well at the end maybe a little bit. And when I was, the most remarkable thing happened. My life passed before my eyes. Not everything. Just the highlights. Kind of like a trailer. I only saw the things that mattered. And I am here to tell you, not one catering job came up. But that damned pottery vase was right there. Front and fucking center.

MISSY. Why are you telling me—?

SPAZ. Use me as your example. Gaze into the portrait, Dorian Gray.

MISSY. You're not that bad.

SPAZ. I'm that bad. There was a time when I lived for love. The mere mention of a possible romance and I was at a mirror practicing my come hither stare. But then came a lot of affairs that didn't hold up in the morning light. And then when people who did love started getting a real ugly disease, I figured I, like Miss Karen Carpenter, would say goodbye to love. I would put my passions in my work. And when that grew tired, I would put my passions into making a living. And what did I become?

MISSY. Hollow?

SPAZ. I prefer sophisticated, but sure, hollow. Why not? Now, portrait gazing. We pledged that no-love sorority together. Well, I don't know about you, sister, but I feel unloved and unfulfilled.

MISSY. But love?

SPAZ. Yeah, love. I have so much love to give. Why do I like just refuse?

MISSY. Oh my baby Spaz

SUIT. This is nonsense. Brat, I think you should leave and take Spaz with you.

MISSY. So I should—

SPAZ. Talk to Brat.

MISSY. You think?

SUIT. You don't have to talk to anyone.

SPAZ. What's the harm in a little talk?

MISSY. But my work. It will change.

BRAT. Yeah. That's how come you're an artist. Your work is always a reflection of you.

MISSY. What about my grants?

SPAZ. I'll tell everyone your parent's home movies are homoerotic. Your grants will be pulled so fast your head will spin.

MISSY. But—Goddamn it—I'm successful!

BRAT. Let me tell you something and don't you ever forget it. Success is nothing without someone you love to share it with.

SPAZ. Doesn't Billy Dee Williams say that in *Mahogany?*

MISSY. Yes.

SPAZ. Talk to him.

MISSY. But—

SUIT. Don't!

MISSY. What?

SPAZ. He's just—

SUIT. Shut up! You're betraying your own tribe, Spaz. Are you really telling a guy to leave a guy for girl?

SPAZ. Boys love boys, boys love girls, girls love boys and girls love girls. Love, in whatever combination, is what matters. And anybody who can't groove to that is just working some serious denial.

SUIT. Shut up! Miss, listen. Missy, you are seriously considering a relationship with a guy who has no job right now, no hints of jobs in the future, no security, is an admitted bisexual, at any minute may just desert you for a senate page or an Olympic skater or even another woman. And who knows? Is perhaps carrying a deadly virus that there is no known cure for. And why are you doing this? Because something you saw in an old movie or read in a book says that this might work? That is not reality. Our relationship is reality. Maybe a little cold. Maybe a little too functional. Maybe a little too "check it in the Filofax," but it is reality.

MISSY. Well ... If all that is so obvious and right, why are you so scared?

SUIT. I'm not scared.

MISSY. Then look me in the eye. (*SUIT can't.*) I'm talking to Brat. O.K.. Brat. Talk to me.

BRAT. O.K. I've been working on this speech the whole ride up. I was thinking of starting off with a quote by Brecht. But I'm not doing Brecht anymore. So I'm kind of an actor without a playwright here. No playwright to choose from. So there's no choice but to ... say what I feel. (*Long pause as HE struggles.*) Fuck.

SPAZ. He chose David Mamet.

BRAT. No. This is me. O.K. Miss? Uhm, first off. Everything that Suit said ... is true. I don't have money. Don't have a job. Don't have anything lined up. And ... I am bi. And even though I don't know any senate pages or ice skaters ... well, I mean that's not to say I never will. Or a woman even. And as far as the virus thing goes, well,

I have been tested by modern science and modern science says that I'm virus free. But then again, modern science checks airplanes before they go in the air, so ... So Suit is very much in the right. There's not tons that I'm offering here. Just that—I love you and I know that you love me. And for as long as you want, I will hold you in my arms ... and protect you from this incredibly fucked era that we're trapped in. And ... (*HIS voice is beginning to shake.*) And if you maybe want to hold me and protect me too. Well—(*Through tears.*) that would be O.K. (*HE composes himself, wipes his tears and tries to seem controlled.*) So, uhm, feedback?

MISSY. (*Walks over to him and puts the back of her hand to his cheek.*) Feedback is good here Brat. Real good.

SUIT. What are you doing?

MISSY. I'm not believing this as I'm saying it, but I'm going with Brat.

SUIT. What about us?

MISSY. I think we're over.

SUIT. Missy—are—it's—don't you think it's insane just changing haphazardly as you see fit?

MISSY. "Not a bit," said the caterpillar.

SPAZ. Not a bit.

SUIT. Everyone in this house is insane but me. Missy, you are just seriously insane here. Why are you leaving with him?

MISSY. (*Casually and sweetly.*) I love him. I have to go now. Bye bye. This has been great. Getting out of the city? We have to do this more often. (*SHE opens the door.*)

SUIT. You're both fools.

MISSY. Well, in this age of great wisdom, maybe two fools will be refreshing.

SUIT. Fools! Two complete fools!
MISSY. You ready, fool number one?
BRAT. Let's go, fool number two.

(THEY exit.)

SUIT. Idiots!! Foolish fucking fools!

(SPAZ begins to laugh.)

SUIT. Just like morons. Total morons.

(SPAZ laughs uproariously.)

SUIT. What are you laughing at? This is all your fault!

(SPAZ is overcome with laughter.)

SUIT. What are you laugh—you're laughing at me aren't you?
SPAZ. Yes. *(HE is laughing wildly.)*
SUIT. I can't believe—I—*(SUIT looks as if HE is going to explode or cry or feel something. Instead HE sits down, closes his eyes and ...)* Adams, Adams, Arthur, Buchanan, Bush, Carter, Cleveland, Coolidge, Fillmore –

(This is too much. Through SPAZ's yelps we hear ...)

SPAZ. Eisenhower.
SUIT. Right. Eisenhower, Fillmore, uh Ford, ...

(SPAZ is laughing merrily as the CURTAIN FALLS.)

End of Play

COSTUME PLOT
Act I

Quick changes are essential to the movement of the play. Many pieces are preset on the stage and added—or subrtracted—during the action. This is described in the following plot.

Scene 1
MISSY
(Underdressed under blanket)
black boots
black all-in-one bustiere
nude sheer hose
black matte hose (worn over nude)
black stirrup pants (worn over both pair of hose)
Multistrand silver bracelet
Silver heart bracelet
Silver peace earrings

SUIT
(During action he puts on the following)
striped boxer shorts
wedding band
Rolex watch
burgandy and grey striped shirt
dark grey 2-piece single breasted suit
black dress belt
burgandy paisley tie
black slip-on shoes
black, grey, burgundy paisley socks

Scene 2
MISSY
(During music she removes sheet, repeats everything from
    I-l and adds:)
pink blouse
black headband with orange flower
red handbag

(During action she adds:)
black watch with pink face and attached bracelet
black rubber bracelet
black coat with pink lining

SPAZ
white Dr. Marten boots
white socks
white underwear
dark oversized jeans
black belt with small buckle
white Robert Longo t-shirt
round glasses
silver hoop earring andpink triangle earring
silver bracelets
Scene 3
MISSY
(During music before scene, she removes headband and adds
    black straw hat and repeats all)
Scene 4
MISSY
(Repeats:)
black boots
sheer hose

black matte hose
stirrup pants
bustiere
silver bracelets
(Adds:)
printed stretch one-piece jumpsuit
green ball drop earrings
barbecue cookout apron
SPAZ
(Repeats:)
underwear
socks
round glasses
(Adds:)
black stud earring
grey painted earing
silver necklace
floral boots
white jeans
black belt with silver buckle and rings
apron
green striped turtle neck
denim shirt with "LOVE" appliqued across front
BRAT
necklace with cross and St. Genesius medal
peace ring
tan underwear
comforter (see props)
Scene 5
MISSY
(Repeats:)
black matte hose

sheer hose
black bustiere
(Adds:)
kimono
SUIT
(Enters wearing:)
blue Nautica robe
off-white boxer shorts
burgandy and black patterned knee-high socks
(During action he removes robes and puts on:)
(Repeats:)
wedding band
watch
(Adds:)
light grey single breasted 2-piece suit
light plaid dress shirt
gray and eggplant dress tie
gray and black suspenders (buttoned into pant)
oxblood slip-on shoes
Scene 6
MISSY
(Repeats:)
black matte hose
sheer hose
bustiere
(Adds:)
black pumps
brown velvet dress
gold and copper earrings
copper pleated shawl
BRAT
(Repeats:)

underwear
jewelry
(Adds:)
black paratrooper boots
white socks
black jeans
black belt with large silver buckle
beige mock turtle
brown corduroy jacket
Scene 7
MISSY
(repeats I-6)
SUIT
(Repeats:)
wedding band
watch
(Adds:)
black slip on-shoes
long burgandy and black patterned socks
navy pant
green and tan paisley suspenders
blue and white striped shirt
tan and rust paisley tie
tan, gray and brown Prince of Wales jacket
sunglasses
underwear
athletic T-shirt
Scene 8
MISSY
(Repeats:)
sheer hose
black hose

black pumps
black bustiere
(Adds:)
green jacket with attached pleated skirt
silver purse
silver paisley earrings
SUIT
(Repeats:)
pant
shoes
socks
suspenders
shirt
watch
wedding band
underwear
athletic T-shirt
(Adds:)
Blue patterned tie
navy double breasted jacket (matches pant)
BRAT
(Repeats:)
underwear
socks
jewelry belt
boot s
(Adds:)
Levi 501 jeans
blue rayon shirt
purple wool jacket
SPAZ
(Repeats:)

underwear
socks
necklace
glasses
(Adds:)
hoop earring
diamond ring
black boots
white shirt with velcro tab at neck
copper and black velvet motor cycle jacket
black pants
thin black belt with silver buckle
Scene 10
MISSY
(Repeats:)
black boots
sheer hose
black bustiere
(Adds:)
black stretch dress with zipper
pink, orange and red motorcycle jacket
pink, orange and red multi-bead chain necklace
SUIT
(Repeats:)
watch
wedding ring
athletic T-shirt
blue pants & suspenders (down on either side of waist)
During scene he starts to add blue & white striped shirt and
    tan & rust paisley tie, then removes at end of scene

BRAT
(Repeats:)
socks
underwear
jewelry
boots
jeans
belt
(Adds:)
red T-shirt
black motorcycle jacket with peace pin
SPAZ
(Repeats:)
socks
pants
belt
glasses
jewelry
(Adds:)
two-piece silk pajamas with "coffee nosh" pattern
silk robe with junk food pattern
Scene 11
MISSY
(Repeats:)
nude hose
(adds:)
white canvas sling back shoes
white dress with gingham applique
natural straw and horsehair hat
natural straw bag
white, pink and red floral earrings
red plastic bracelet

BRAT
(Repeats:)
socks
underwear
jeans
jewelry
(Adds during action of scene:)
Nike sneakers
gray hooded tank top
Scene 12
SPAZ
(Repeats:)
socks
underwear
glasses
jewelry
black belt (from I-2)
(Adds:)
black boots
Levi 501 jeans
red bandana T—shirt
black rubber raincoat with Act Up pin
jughead hat
SUIT
(Repeats:)
I-5 outfit
(Adds:)
tan raincoat

ACT II

<u>Scene 1</u>
SPAZ
(Repeats:)
underwear
jewelry (I-2)
glasses
Levi 501 jeans (I-12)
(Adds:)
mood ring
brown cowboy boots
two-tone socks
brown belt with silver buckle
white shirt with embroidery
Indian blanket coat
orange scarf and bolo tie
SUIT
suede slip-on shoes
tan socks
khaki trousers
burgundy coach belt
red long sleeve polo shirt
denim shirt
tan, brown and red patterned sweater (worn over shoulders)
underwear
brown leather watch band
wedding ring
(During action he removes sweater and adds:) green baseball
    hat
brown flack jacket
MISSY
Green leather flats

sheer hose
black stretch capri pants
nude bra with straps
white stretch tank
pink and orange striped silk blouse
orange fish print doo rag
gold drop earrings
sunglasses, motorcycle jacket from I-10
(During action she removes sunglasses and motorcycle
    jacket from I-10)
BRAT
(Repeats:)
Nike sneakers
socks
jeans
jewelry
(Add:)
high school OLPS (Our Lady of Perpetual Sorrow)
    letterman's jacket with name "Tony" embroidered and
    misc patches on sleeves
hooded short sleeve shirt
Scene 2
MISSY
same as II-1
BRAT
(At top of scene he is wearing:)
turquoise underwear
white terry robe
(During action he adds II-1 outfit)
SUIT
(Repeats:)
watch

underwear
shoes
wedding ring
(Adds:)
green and tan argyle socks
moss green trousers
tan and green striped suspenders
Indian plaid shirt
blue cotton cardigan
SPAZ
(Repeats:)
socks
underwear
jewelry
glasses
floral boots (I-4)
(Adds:)
overalls
yellow and tan striped sweater

FURNITURE AND PROPS

However you do the unit set for Act One you will probably
want to incorporate the following:

<u>Missy's Bedroom</u>
1 bed
1 set of sheets and pillow cases
2 pillows
<u>Spaz's Kitchen</u>
1 counter (oven underneath)
2 stools
shelves
1 chair
<u>Radio Station</u>
1 table
1 chair
1 "on the air" sign
<u>Art Gallery</u>
1 huge blowup photo of Missy's face
<u>Restaurant</u>
1 table with table cloth
4 chairs
<u>Train station</u>
1 Amtrak sign "Hudson"

Prop List
Act I

<u>Scene 1</u>
cigarette
lighter
portable ashtray

attaché case
Scene 2
pottery vase
Scene 3
microphone headset
Scene 4
3 mixing bowls
4 small plates
1 creamer (1/2 full w/milk)
1 sugar bowl
2 coffee mugs
     (all preferably fiestaware)
2 small roasting pans
2 large roasting pans
4 fake croissants
1 real croissant (broken in 3 places)
2 fake hens
4 oven mits
2 aprons
1 baster (with brown fluid)
1 coffee maker (1/2 full)
1 egg timer
3 serving utensils
1 bag of flour
1 jar of preserves
1 comforter
Scene 5
1 Wall Street Journal
Scene 6
plastic champagne glasses (1/2 full w/flat ginger ale)
Scene 7
1 filofax

1 cordless telephone
3 magazines
2 pens
Scene 8
4 plastic champagne glasses
1 bottle of champagne (1/2 full w/flat ginger ale)
4 menus
1 champagne bucket
1 champagne bucket stand
1 ashtray
1 pack of cigarettes
1 lighter
Scene 10
1 lap computer
1 slip of paper with time of train
1 fiestaware bowl (1/2 full of popcorn)
1 can of soda
1 *New York Times* crossword puzzle
1 pencil
Scene 11
1 "boom box"
1 black leather shoulder bag
1 pr. sunglasses
1 beach towel
1 book (preferably Brecht)
1 wicker suitcase
Scene 12
1 umbrella

Act II

1 copy of *Alice in Wonderland*

1 quilt
2 cups of coffee
1 game of *Candyland*
1 bottle of Corona beer (filled with flat ginger ale)
1 pack of cigarettes
1 ashtray
1 lighter
1 fishing rod
1 life preserver
1 oar
1 laundry basket

The Act Two set for the New York production was filled
with the following:
1 sofa
1 wingback chair
1 Shaker chair
1 trunk (as a coffee table)
1 sideboard
1 side table
1 shaker pegboard
1 twig basket
1 braided basket
assorted artificial fruit
1 lamp
1 fireplace
andirons
fireplace tools
1 green pitcher
2 throw pillows
1 fish basket
1 fish net

1 fish trap
4 antique milk bottles
3 tin boxes
1 fabric swag (over the window)
various kid's games
1 ship model
3 decoys
3 stuffed animals
childrens books
hardback books

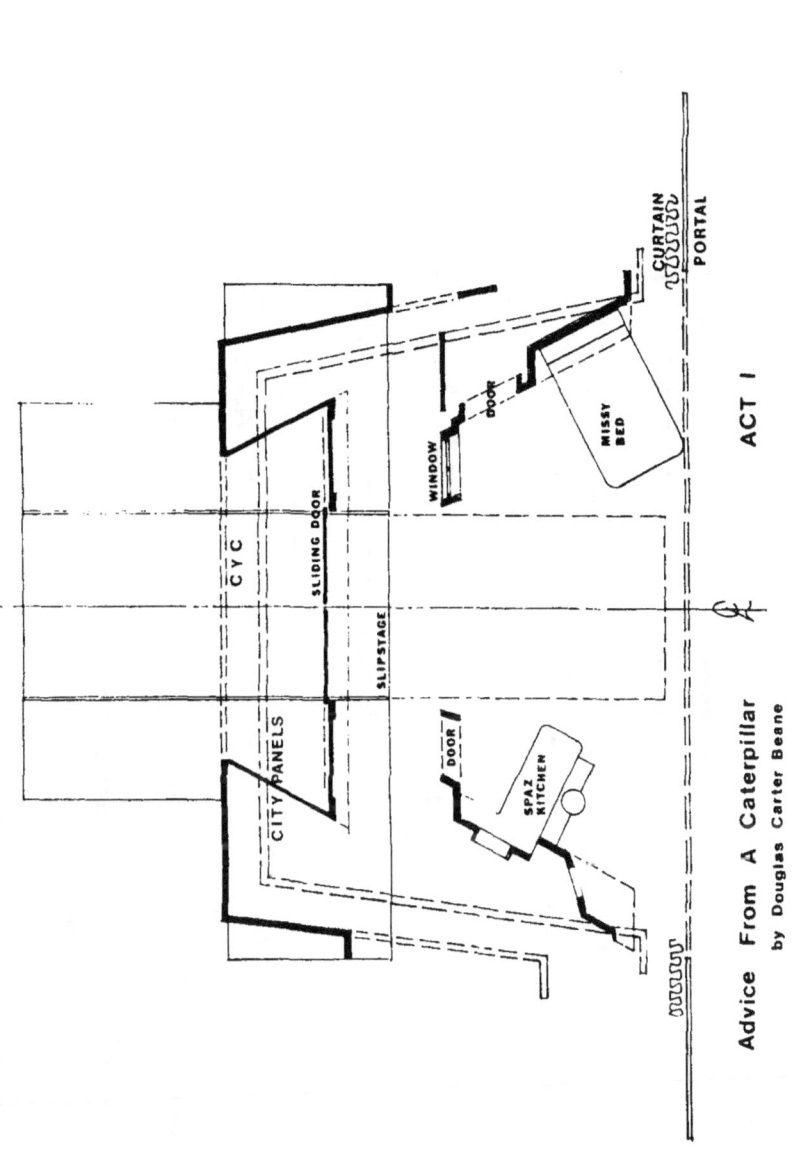

Advice From A Caterpillar
by Douglas Carter Beane

ACT I

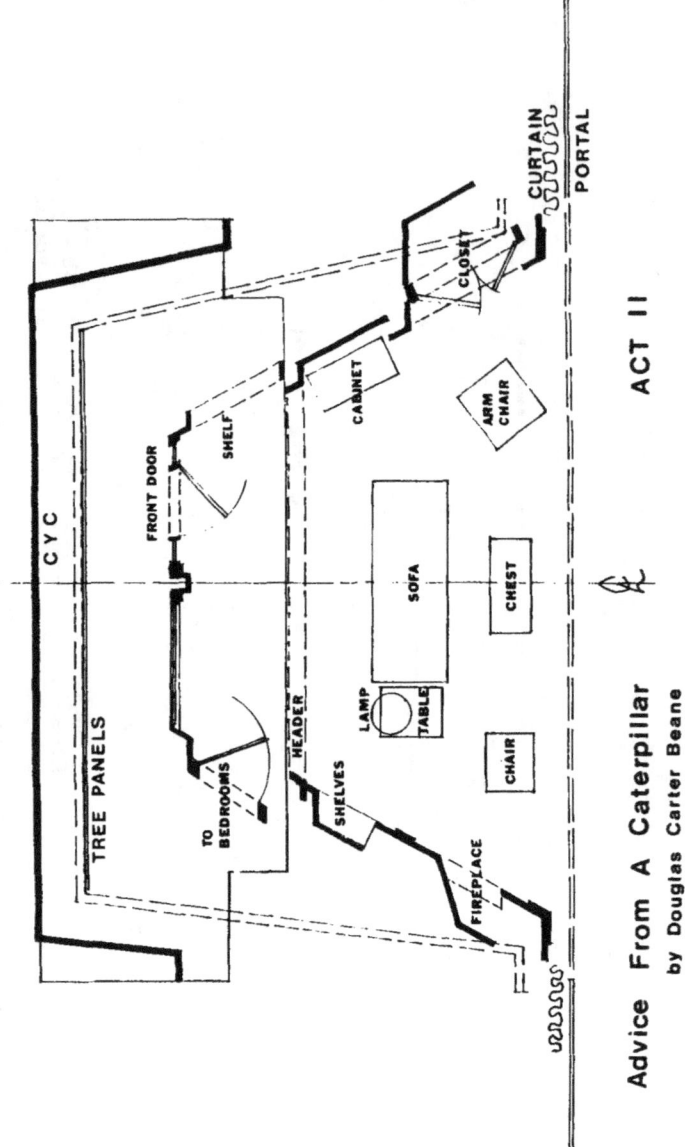

Advice From A Caterpillar

by Douglas Carter Beane

ACT II